Charles Grafton Page

Psychomancy; Spirit-Rappings and Table-Tippings Exposed

in large print

AF130292

Charles Grafton Page

Psychomancy; Spirit-Rappings and Table-Tippings Exposed

in large print

Reproduction of the original.

1st Edition 2023 | ISBN: 978-3-38708-080-3

Megali Verlag is an imprint of Outlook Verlagsgesellschaft mbH.

Verlag (Publisher): Outlook Verlag GmbH, Zeilweg 44, 60439 Frankfurt, Deutschland
Vertretungsberechtigt (Authorized to represent): E. Roepke, Zeilweg 44, 60439 Frankfurt, Deutschland
Druck (Print): Books on Demand GmbH, In de Tarpen 42, 22848 Norderstedt, Deutschland

PSYCHOMANCY

SPIRIT-RAPPINGS AND TABLE-TIPPINGS

EXPOSED

BY

PROF. CHARLES G. PAGE,

1853

SPIRIT-RAPPINGS.

The wide-spread and alarming mania of *Spirit-rappings* and *table-tippings* of the present day, is only a modification, or new garb, of *devilish instrumentalities*, operating through human machinations, which have infested society from time immemorial. We start with this proposition, harsh as it may sound to some, and if we should fail to sustain it by facts, reasoning, and common sense, to the entire satisfaction of all, we still say to the unbelievers in our doctrine, show us the proof to the contrary; and with a confidence firm as our belief in Holy Writ, and the unfailing laws of God, we challenge the exhibition to our senses of any performance with spirit-rappings, or table-tippings, which cannot be explained upon natural, and *well known* natural laws. We will here premise, that we do not attribute to Satan any direct agency in this matter other than has always been ascribed to him in the crimes and misdeeds of man from the fall down to this present time. That neither the "prince of the power of the air," nor his imps (unless they be in human shape), rap out intelligence by sounds, get under tables and tip them over, swing them round, or perform any of these extraordinary feats, which so many among us are determined to invest with supernatural character and origin. Nor do we consider that the arch-enemy of man has brought any *new power* or *agency* into operation to further his mischievous designs. FAR FROM IT. *A new power?* It would frustrate his schemes in their very inception. *A new power?* It is a lawful subject of pursuit, to the very exhaustion of mental resources. *A new power?* Its bare mention is an arousing signal to the devotees of science, and upon the first scintillation of plausibility, the midnight lamp will burn throughout Christendom, till its capabilities and subserviency to man's actual wants are unfolded. No! the tempter knows his game and tools, and perhaps his own limits, all too well to give to man a new and legitimate object of research, and thus divert investigation from hallucinating and mercenary sorceries to that which is lawful and truthful. He works with his own and old tools, upon and through that most successful instrumentality, over which, by long and dire experience, he has acquired such mighty ascendency— the human soul. This is his pliant tool, and here his stronghold. To those who regard the Scriptural account of the devil's existence and agency as allegorical, our argument, in its cardinal character and bearing, will apply with the same force, for they have only to invest the mind of man with all the force and attributes that the allegory gives to both combined, and we address ourselves to them with the same interest and hope of success as with those who believe the Scripture implicitly to the letter. To all alike, the deep, untiring, unending wiles of the human soul are familiar themes, and it matters but little to our present purpose,

4

whether these impious transactions proceed from the main-spring of unaided, uninspired thought, or whether the unheeding thought is impressed by supernal powers. There is in the mind a strong and often morbid appetency for the supernatural and marvellous; a proneness to inquire beyond what is actually revealed; and, worse than this, a prurience of power, either real or specious, to exalt one above his fellow mortals, and give the weight of Divine authority to his words and acts. From this desire originates priestcraft, astrology and sorcery, and in the former habitude of the mind lies the secret of their success and perpetuation. It has been a real source of distress to us, to see professing Christians, even among our immediate friends, pushing their inquiries beyond the confines of realities into the spirit-world, forgetting or misapprehending the injunctions of Scripture forbidding us to look into such things, and unconscious of the fact, that their well-meant invocations of spirits by the tipping of tables and rappings, was, in every step and act of repetition, lending encouragement to the mercenary and nefarious schemes of a certain set of vile impostors, who originated the cheat, and were continuing its practice for the sake of filthy lucre. To them, and to all, we say Stop! ere this temerity be visited with the righteous judgments of an offended Deity, who has pronounced, in his holy oracles, in clear and unmistakable language, his malediction of sorcery and witchcraft; has set the bounds of human inquiry where time stops and eternity begins, and sealed up the future in impenetrable mystery; who has refused to the yearning hearts of fond and bereaved parents all knowledge of their dear departed, save the hopes and consolations of the Scripture. What! shall the GREAT JUDGMENT be anticipated, and the archives of eternal retribution be read by the *knocking of sticks upon the floor*, or the upsetting of tables? Shall eternity be made subordinate to time; the immortal to the mortal? Shall the silence of the grave be disturbed by grovelling mountebanks, or its stern abodes become vocal through these gross mediums of rappers and tippers? IMPIOUS! IMPIOUS! We need not quote Scripture against this unholy pursuit, for its anathemas are full and loud, and he who runs may read. We know there are those who are innocently engaged in the *invocation of* spirits, and who seem to take delight in holding converse with their departed friends, as they suppose. We ask them to pause, and consider well what they are doing! to look around, and see the devastation of human intellect, the fearful swellings of the madhouse rolls, the frightful deeds of blood and violence, and the stupendous frauds, all begotten of this monster mania! Are these the fruits of legitimate and holy deeds? Are these your consolations while at your spiritual shrines? Do they not bear evidence in themselves of their diabolical origin, and are they not warnings to you to beware, lest in your attempts to enter beyond the veil into the "*Holy of Holies*," you be struck down also? If these pests of society are beyond the reach of earthly tribunals, will you countenance and encourage their career? Shall we be met here with the assertion that there are religious maniacs, that religious excitement makes madmen, and leads to deeds of violence? We spurn the fallacy; and with proud defiance, armed with the Rock of Ages, we hurl back the apology in the very teeth of the casuist who made it, and, fearless of his replication, triumphantly assert that the true religion of Jesus Christ, whose first fruits and very essence is peace to the soul, NEVER DROVE ANY BODY MAD.

We profess a profound reverence for all that is holy, and from our earliest recollection have been imbued with a deep dread of profanity in any shape, and approached this mockery of high Heaven with some reluctance, unwilling that our veneration should suffer so much violence. But we felt justified, in the full assurance that this thing was not of Heaven, but of men. For the sake of unravelling this imposture and illusion, for this purpose *alone*, we have put ourselves frequently in the attitude of dupes of these impostors, and feigning for a time conviction and conversion, have led them on till they were completely baffled in every attempt to perform their tricks, and the spirits became powerless and silent as the mortal tenements they once actuated. When we first sat down to a table with a few well-meaning and particular family friends to conjure spirits, we confess to a momentary feeling of horripilation, not from fear of meeting a visitor from another world, but from the impression that the very act was *heaven-daring* and *profane*. But when we came to utter the Rapper's Shibboleth, *"If there are any spirits present, will they please to signify it by tipping the table?"* the thoughts of sacrilege vanished, and were immediately supplanted by an irresistible sense of the ridiculous, and the smile and the laugh rose above all convictions of solemnity or irreverence. "Will the spirits please to tip the table?" was again and again reiterated, but no table tipped for us. Perhaps we are not "*mediums*," said one. "The spirits have declared that I am a medium," said another; but that Great Exorcist, *common sense*, was present and prevalent on this occasion; and the spirits would not communicate, and the table would not tip, *certainly not, of itself*. We introduced every variety of manipulation of crossing hands, interlocking fingers, and, in spite of all, and the most patient persistence, the table proved true to its lifeless character, and the universal law that "*matter is inert, and cannot move of itself*." What could have been the cause of this abortive conjuration? Were the spirits present, and not disposed to gratify a certain class of *dilettanti* who were present? Were they jesting and teazing, or in bad humor with our persons, our fixtures, or our espionage? For we had heard from very respectable sources, of the spirits jesting and taunting those present on such occasions. Or were they far away on some errand of duty, or busy and monopolized for some *special tippings* elsewhere? This last idea seems to be precluded by the fact that certain great spirits, such as Channing, Webster, Clay and Calhoun, who figure so largely on these occasions, rap and tip in different places at the same time. What mummery is all this to the mind that believes in the omnipresence of the Great God himself, who cannot look upon such practices but with abhorrence. Are you, Christian man or woman, one whit better for these doings than that woman with the familiar spirits, the Witch of Endor?[1] Are you not rather her disciple? and is she not held up to you for an example and a warning? Do you think that rappings and table-tippings give respectability to witchcraft? Is reading the future and the invisible world by rappings and tippings any better than the doings of yonder wretched crone, who works out in her concealed abode the same problems by packs of cards and mystical incantations? Are you not ministering encouragement to her hagship, and pursuing her very vocation, though under another name? Shall not this veritable beldame rise up in judgment, and plead in justification of *fortune-telling* the example of the Christian Church in spirit-rapping and table-tipping? Perhaps you think that these seeming wonders are fraught with more interest, novelty, and mystery, than the magical demonstrations of old. Why, in very truth, they are contemptibly insignificant when compared with the witcheries of old. Read Upham's letters on the witchcraft of the New England Colonies, Sir Walter Scott's demonology and witchcraft, and see how the rappings and tippings dwindle before the performances of the witches of yore. After reading these, study well Sir David Brewster's Natural Magic—a book that should be in the hands of every one who takes interest in these marvels of the day. There you will see how phenomena, at first sight inexplicable, are solved by the touch-stones of science and common sense. You will there find that sorcery was not to be stopped entirely by the gibbet, the gallows or the stake, but that the light of reason and science were most effectual in promoting its overthrow. Sir Walter Scott says of the opposers of witchcraft in the seventeenth century, that the "pursuers of exact science to its coy retreats were sure to be the first to discover that the most remarkable phenomena in nature are regulated by certain fixed laws, and cannot be rationally referred to supernatural agency" (meaning, of course, supernatural interference), "the sufficing cause to which superstition attributes all that is beyond her own narrow power of explanation. Each advance in natural knowledge teaches us, that it is the pleasure of the Creator to govern the world by the laws which he has imposed, and which in our times are not interrupted or suspended."

In all ages, the Church has attributed sorcery to the agency of the devil. If this is his work, he certainly proceeds upon the same general *modus operandi* as ever. As one artifice wears out, or is exploded by the power of science, he resorts to another; that is, he prompts new tricks by his own unseen influences, upon the minds of those who become his willing instruments. The most gross of all is spirit-rapping, and next, the subtle delusions of mesmerism, and table-tippings. We cannot stop here to discuss mesmerism, for whatever there may be in it of lawful inquiry, surely the sending of clairvoyant spirits to the portals of heaven or hell, to bring back descriptions of those abodes and their inhabitants, is sorcery of the most impious character. Some years ago said a distinguished poet, "Satan now, is wiser than of yore;" doubtless he has advanced a few degrees in strategy, since Pope's time, and as the light and power of science and wisdom increase, so does he deepen his plots and shift his points of attack. Now we will repeat here, that it is entirely immaterial to our purpose whether our readers believe in the seen or unseen, direct or indirect influences of the devil upon mind or matter, or in neither one nor the other. If they do not believe that he "goes about like a roaring lion, seeking whom he may devour," if they do not believe in the existence of such a malignant being, they have only this alternative, that they must find the devil's equivalent in the human heart, which though a less palatable doctrine, will answer the design of this argument, which is to show that these pretended wonders of knocks and table movements are

11

illusory, nefarious and mischievous, originating chiefly from evil-minded persons, and perpetuated by the indifference of careless observers, the connivance of others, and mainly by the fanaticism, ignorance, and credulousness of a large class of persons found in every community. These have been recognized in all ages as the principal ingredients in sorcery, but there is yet another element which is doing much to foster this crime, and although not a new feature, yet is quite prevalent at this time, and less excusable than it was in the days of Bacon and Napier. Sir Walter Scott, in one of his letters, has this point in our discussion so strongly portrayed, that we take the liberty of quoting him at some length, rejoicing in the opportunity of adding his great wisdom and authority in these matters, to our own efforts. Speaking of the causes which retarded the subversion of witchcraft in the sixteenth and seventeenth centuries, among learned men, he says, "The learned and sensible Dr. Webster, for instance, writing in the detection of the supposed witchcraft, assumes, as a string of undeniable facts, opinions which our more experienced age would reject as frivolous fancies; for example, the effects of healing by the weapon-salve, the sympathetic powder, the curing of various diseases by apprehensions, amulets, or by transplantation." All of which undoubted wonders he accuses the age of desiring to throw on the devil's back—an unnecessary load, certainly, since such things do not exist, and it is therefore in vain to seek to account for them. It followed, that while the opposers of the ordinary theory might have struck the deepest blow at the witch hypothesis by an appeal to common sense, they were themselves hampered by articles of philosophical belief, which, they must have been sensible, contained nearly as deep draughts upon human credulity as were made by the demonologists, against whose doctrine they protested. This error had a doubly bad effect, both as degrading the immediate department in which it occurred, and as affording a protection for falsehood in other branches of science. The champions who, in their own province, were obliged by the imperfect knowledge of the times to admit much that was mystical and inexplicable; those who opined, with Bacon, that warts could be cured by sympathy—who thought, with Napier, that hidden treasure could be discovered by the mathematics—who salved the weapon instead of the wound, and detected murders as well as springs of water by the divining-rod, could not consistently use, to confute the believers in witches, an argument turning on the impossible or the incredible.

"Such were the obstacles arising from the vanity of philosophers and the imperfection of their science, which suspended the strength of their appeal to reason and common sense, against the condemning of wretches to a cruel death, on account of crimes, which the nature of things rendered in modern times impossible."

Thus learned men seeking to unravel mysteries, for want of sagacity and full knowledge, may become the apologists of sorcery and witchcraft. Bacon was obliged to be a philosopher for the whole enlightened world; but, in our day, so vast has each branch of science become, that any one of them would be full enough for a Bacon's grasp, and philosophers hardly dare to venture outside of their own boundaries, lest they become, or be considered *philosophists*. We hear men of science abused because they take such obstinate, inexorable positions against these "*fooleries.*" This they are bound to do. Familiar with the laws of nature, all real phenomena are alike marvellous to their minds, and those which claim to be miraculous, supernatural, and, *par excellence*, the MARVELLOUS, they repudiate summarily as absurdities, knowing that if they cannot disabuse the popular mind, they can prove their irrationality to their own entire satisfaction, at least. Formerly fortune-tellers were sometimes styled Philomaths, but we think that as fortune-telling has degenerated into such disrepute, the name is unworthily applied, and we propose to transfer it to that class of learned writers of the present day, who seek to trace these tricks of raps and tips to the direct agency of the devil, or evil or good spirits;—supposing these spirits to make the sounds or movements, and to give the communications;— and to that class specially who attribute these phenomena to electricity, magnetism, or to the action of some power or fluid hitherto unknown; in short, to all, who look upon these things as any thing else than impostures and illusions. These are the philomaths of the present day, and while they thus stand in the way of advancement in true knowledge, they are, in effect, fostering error, superstition, and sorcery. We boast in our day of the enlightenment of the masses, the spread of education and the diffusion of knowledge; but for all this, necromancy is not dead nor stifled; and is now like a baleful poison running rife through our land, upon the most preposterous foundations and pretexts. Spirits, rapping upon doors, floors, and tables, upsetting tables and swinging them about the room? Spirits, do you say? Has a "spirit flesh and blood?" Has a spirit *bones, muscles, fingers, heels, toes, and sticks*? Do SPIRITS WEAR PETTICOATS *and long dresses*? A "*new fluid*," says another philomath. A new fluid, forsooth? None other than that old fluid of credulity or gullibity, if we may be allowed the latter term. An "old fluid," says another. "Electricity or magnetism in some shape." This is insufferable. Since the first discoveries in electricity and magnetism, these agents have had to take the paternity of every rare and inexplicable phenomenon. This is much more the case now than when Sir Walter Scott wrote his letters on witchcraft, though he says that the divining-rod, and other remarkable and misconceived phenomena, were assigned to the agency of electricity and magnetism. At the present times these subtle agents are the common *scape-goats* for mesmeric, electro-biological, psychological, and every other kind of phenomenon, the cause of which eludes the senses, and the new-fangled farce of "rappings and tippings" must fain take advantage of the same subterfuge in order to make its way to popular credence. Unfortunately, in this case an accurate knowledge of the laws of electricity is possessed by comparatively few persons; and the electric fluid, or power of magnetism, becomes a very clever instrument in the hands of charlatans and empirics, through which to enforce upon the popular mind the reality of their tricks and impostures. To one who has an adequate knowledge of the laws of electricity and magnetism, it is more than amusing to see with what pedantic gravity these latter philomaths descant upon electricity and magnetism, contorting and butchering their established laws all the while, to explain some vile juggle, or unravel the psychomancy of rappers and tippers; and also to see with what avidity their inflated arguments are gulped by gaping crowds, who apparently are unwilling or unable to swallow a single *naked truth*. It is often said that "men love to be deceived." This is true to some extent, and it is sometimes the case that a quack will draw crowds around him where a truly learned man could not get a foothold. The truth however is mighty, and will prevail, and the power of learning always has been, and will be felt, though it may be somewhat slow to assert and maintain its supremacy. In verity, there is not one property, condition, or law of electricity or magnetism, so far as they have been established by experiment and science, that would explain rappings and tippings without doing violence to philosophy. A few years ago, a medical friend and brother came to our house late at night, in considerable trepidation, and wished us to go and see a woman who was bewitched in an extraordinary manner. At intervals she would be seized with convulsions, and while the fit was on her she pulled pins out of the hands, arms, and legs of bystanders, and tossing the pins into her mouth, swallowed them. We remonstrated with him, but though highly intelligent, and excelling in his profession, our friend the Doctor would not give it up. He had seen it, believed it, but could not account for it, and came to us specially to ascertain if "ELECTRICITY had not something to do with it." Knowing that the witches of old had a special fancy for pins, and fully prepared to see nothing more than a dexterous feat of legerdemain, we consented to go, late as it was, and as soon as the pretty little elf, who was lying upon a pallet upon the floor, had become convulsed, and pulled a pin from our person, and swallowed it, we discovered the *quomodò*, and the next day, with a little practice, we were able to go into very fair convulsions, and could draw out pins and swallow them as skilfully as the witch herself. Our good friend, the doctor, had not even noticed that the convulsive movements were all confined to the voluntary actions upon the muscles, so engrossed was he

17

with the idea of the supernatural character of this performance. It is remarkable to notice how the scrutinizing powers of the most astute, fail as soon as they entertain the remotest idea of the supernatural in these cases. This girl was visited by hundreds of respectable and intelligent persons in our community, and notwithstanding a publication which was made exposing the trick, but few were able to discover it for themselves, and the greater portion believed it to be a genuine performance, and alms were freely given in sympathy for her unfortunate condition. Our sympathies were enlisted for those whom *she bewitched*, and we must give the *enchantress* credit for more shrewdness than her customers, and we believe she reaped quite a rich harvest for her skill in legerdemain. We cite this case to show what violence is done to science to account for modern sorceries. *Remember*, we are called on to decide if *electricity* played any part in this extraordinary exhibition.

Many years ago a person of the name of Hannington came to Salem, Massachusetts, then the place of our residence, to exhibit the so-called *mysterious lady*. This lady had the power of naming and describing various things which she could not see, declare names written upon bits of paper handed to persons promiscuously in the audience, and a variety of performances, which completely astounded her visitors. Their programme announced that they had visited the principal cities in this country and Europe, and that her extraordinary gift of divination had baffled the ablest researches. We were invited to see this great modern Pythoness, and specially for the purpose of judging whether it was an *auricular* illusion. In a word, whether it might not be an extraordinary case of ventriloquism, for this seems to have been the last resort for a solution of the problem, with those who repudiated witchery. Electricity would not answer this time, and the science of sound had to be mutilated for the occasion. Being ourselves expert in the performance of ventriloquism, and familiar with the laws of acoustics, it needed but a moment to decide that ventriloquism was utterly inadequate to the solution of the puzzle, and before we left the room we discerned the whole trick, disconcerted the performers very essentially, and the next day published a full exposure, after which the whereabouts of the *mysterious lady* was a greater mystery than her performances had been.

A few years since, an account was published throughout this country and Europe, of a prodigy in the shape of an *electrical girl* in Paris, who was indued with an extraordinary power—*electrical* of course—by which, when she attempted to sit down in a chair, it was thrown from her with great violence. This was one of the wonders of the day, and after having deceived multitudes, and become an object of universal interest and sympathy, she fell into the hands of a select committee of the Academy of Sciences, with Arago at their head. Does any one suppose that Arago ever entertained for a moment the idea of electrical action in this connection? Not at all! Arago immediately set himself to the examination of the girls heels, and soon found that she moved the chairs by muscular effort. By long practice she had acquired such skill and power of kicking, or thrusting the chair away from herself, that it was always done without exhibiting any motion exterior to her dress, or the slightest disturbance of her person. So much for electricity or the "*new fluid*" in this case. This kicking girl was styled the *Electrical girl*, or the *Electrical wonder*. Of course she belonged to the *new fluid class*, for no one acquainted with the laws of electricity, would have entertained a suspicion that electricity had any thing to do with the phenomenon.

We may be accused of being somewhat dogmatical in this treatise, and perhaps we are so, while we have to deal with so many fanatics and pragmatical philomaths. For the superstitious and ignorant, we have some charity, but we confess that we have little or no patience for those among educated men, who are wearers of the *amulets* of electricity, magnetism, or *new fluids*. They evince more pedantry than penetration, and are inexcusable disseminators of sophistry and error. They are exactly in the category of the believers in perpetual motion, and, in fact, the ascription of such phenomena as table-tippings to electricity, magnetism, or some new fluid, goes a step beyond perpetual motion, if that is possible. Most of the plodders after perpetual motion expect to get, by some new adjustment, a machine that will barely move of itself without any great surplus of power; but according to this new table-tipping philosophy, we certainly should look for any amount of horse power, without any consumption of material, and no other expense than that of keeping a clever medium at hand. On the principle of touching a heavy table *lightly* (for the touch must be light according to rule), and thus causing by incantations the table to tip, rise up, whirl about, etc., it would cost but little to move a church or a mountain, and mediums should be in great demand for mechanical purposes, as being cheaper and safer than steam engines. How strange it does appear, that these pseudo-philosophers have entirely lost sight of the one great radical principle of all dynamic science, viz., that action and reaction are equal, and never have attached the least value to the fact, that when persons put their hands *lightly* upon tables, *their hands always follow the motion of the table, whichever way the table moves.* It certainly appeared to us a very *significant* fact, when we first saw the performance, and if considered in connection with electricity, or the *new fluid*, is sufficiently anomalous to require a careful analysis. But more of this anon, as we propose to examine the rappings first. This imposture originated with two girls, by the name of Fox, from Rochester, New-York, who are now, with their mother, travelling through the country, and exhibiting their art for money. A few weeks ago, the Fox-mother gave us an account of this wonderful development of noises or rappings about the two daughters, and from her we learned that the noises were kept up for a long time before they discovered the cause. At first they were annoyed by them, but, *after a while,* they became so familiar with the sounds, that they took but little notice of them, until they discovered the mode of communicating with their authors, and ascertained that the sounds were made by spirits of the departed. According to her account, the spirits then rapped at points remote from the girls, but it seems that the spiritual habit has changed somewhat, for since the girls have been on exhibition,[2] the spirits rap nowhere except directly *under the girls, and about their feet,* or upon something with which their persons or dresses are in contact. We had no desire to see these creatures, except to discover the precise means by which they made the raps, and although fully prepared to condemn them before we paid them a visit, we preferred not to condemn them unseen, lest, on that ground, the clique of rappers should have some advantage over our argument.

It amuses us greatly at times, when discussing these matters with our friends, to be told that our "opinions are all made up beforehand," "that we are prejudiced," &c. We admit the charge, and say frankly we *are* prejudiced, and mean to prejudge any effort to make black appear to be

22

white, and white, black; and declare the pretensions of these rappers and tippers to be as grossly absurd and silly, as any monstrosity in the shape of a proposition, that ever emanated from a crazy or evil designing brain. When we are told that a table is moved by the mere effort of the will, that it moves about when it is not touched, we deny the statement *flatly* at once, and challenge the reproduction of the miracle, and when we are told that spirits rap upon tables, floors, doors, walls, or any thing else, we deny the statement, and challenge the production of any kind of rap or sound in these cases, which is not clearly traceable to human agency. Perhaps it will be inferred that we either do or should take ground against supernatural interference and miracles altogether, seeing that we are prepared to condemn *à priori*, these manifestations, claiming for themselves supernatural origin. We confess that one of the greatest obstacles we have to encounter in the course of this exposition, is the deep-rooted belief in the existence, at the present day, of miraculous powers, agencies and deeds, and the readiness with which many persons ascribe every thing which eludes their judgment or senses, and especially whatever savors in the least of religion, to superhuman agency. We do not mean to draw upon Holy Writ for arguments in support of our decision, upon these *rappings* and *tippings*, but anticipating the reception we shall meet, with this class of persons, we must advert briefly to the grounds of their belief and objection, and at the same time define our own position. We here find ourselves arrayed against learned divines of the present day, who, failing to account for these strange doings upon the supposition of human agency, resort to their belief in the superhuman, and consistently with their professional calling, must evidently found their views upon scripture. Failing to discern the "*finger of God*," they have come to their last resort, "that these manifestations are the work of the devil, or of evil spirits." Without claiming any depth in biblical lore, we ask them where is the authority for any such conclusion in the Bible? The Bible teaches plainly of the devil's agency, of his operations upon the heart of man, and so far would such a construction be justifiable, but no farther. There is not one instance recorded, in which Satanic agency was recognizable by man as *immediate*. "By their fruits ye shall know them," is a sufficient rule of judgment for any deeds, pretensions, or manifestations whatsoever; and here they should rest content, and instead of going beyond the record, might safely administer the general caution, that these "lies are of their father, the devil," without introducing the whole Pandemonium into our houses, to overturn our tables and upset the laws of gravity and mechanical philosophy. We believe that miracles were performed of old, for holy purposes, and no other; that they were necessary to enforce the truth of revelation; that the day of miracles has gone by, and that they ceased when their necessity ceased. We have our own mode of fixing that period, but the discussion would be too far from our present purpose, and we have digressed too much already. We take the ground that every witch, wizard, magician, astrologer, sorcerer, necromancer, and fortune-teller, from the earliest, down to the present time, has had no more power over matter, or the laws of nature, than any other person, and that whoever lays claim to familiar spirits, foresight, or any direct communication with the invisible world, through raps and tips, is either witch, wizard, conjurer, or sorcerer *de facto*.[3] The prime movers in all these marvels are *impostors*, and their disciples, *dupes*. While the former are filling their coffers at the expense of the latter, they must often indulge in secret merriment at the credulity of their adherents; and particularly at the grave discussions of the learned clergy and others upon electricity, magnetism, the new fluid, the nervous fluid, or the devil's immediate agency, as probable causes of these strange phenomena. Surely the "children of this world are wiser than the children of light." The juggler with his legerdemain far outstrips any thing that has ever been accomplished by rappers and tippers, but then he tells you that he performs by sleight of hand, and that unless your eyes are quicker than his hands, you will be deceived. If certain of his performances were to be introduced with some religious jargon and pretext, his success in infatuating the mass of the people, would put the rappers and tippers entirely in the shade, for the tricks of these latter are clumsy and poorly done at the best. Mr. Anderson, the professed juggler, known as the Wizard of the North, has, to his great credit, published a series of communications, in which he boldly avers that these rappers are all impostors, and has contrived a system of rapping and spiritual communications, quite as successful as those of the original fraternity. He has failed, however, to elucidate the whole subject, from the fact that he has been contented with a mere imitation, which the rappers will of course pronounce a counterfeit. Our first visit to the rappers, was in company with a gentleman of high eminence in science, of keen discernment, and very fruitful in expedients. We had formed no particular plan of procedure, except that we had agreed to feign belief in these performances, lest incredulity might prove an obstacle to investigation, and keep the rappers too much on their guard. Repudiating all idea of the supernatural, we were not liable to any distraction on that account, and our attention was directed entirely to the scrutiny of the performances, with reference to their solution upon established principles of evidence and natural laws. If the advocates of this new "spiritual philosophy" should object to this prejudication, our answer is, that aside from our prior experience in unravelling many such pretended wonders, we hold our position to be entirely justifiable, on the ground of probabilities, and that hitherto we have never known an instance in which so much of presumption was not in such cases, legitimated in the conclusion of facts.

Be this as it may, we had resolved to follow up these rappings and tippings to see whether they were impostures, delusions, or illusions, one or all. After the mother of the Fox girls had given us an account of the spiritual visitation of her daughters, they three took seats at a large circular table, and we joined the circle sitting opposite to them. We were directed to ask if there were any spirits present. This done, BANG, BANG upon the table announced the presence of the spirits. The table was evidently struck underneath by something *hard*, *solid*, *material*, and so as to jar the table perceptibly to the hand resting upon it. Our coadjutor feigned surprise and alarm, and stooped to look under the table, when the raps immediately ceased. This he repeated several times and each time the raps ceased. We asked again if there were any spirits present, but no answer came while he had his eyes below the level of the table top, but as soon as he sat up, the raps upon the table commenced again. He however was so persevering in his scrutiny about the table as to give us a good opportunity to say—for mere effect— "Why do you look under there, you cannot *see* a spirit?" The rappers finding themselves baffled in making their demonstrations through the table, were forced to retreat from it, and taking their seats a short distance from the table, the rappings then commenced upon the floor immediately under the girls, or about their feet. Both the girls were rappers, but one conspicuously so, she rapping much louder than the other, and did most of the rapping for the occasion. Both the girls wore long dresses sweeping the floor, but the principal rapper ought to have been attended by a train bearer. "Are there any spirits present?" was again asked, and the raps came promptly and so thick and fast that the spirits seemed anxious to make some communications, so we proceeded to this part of the ceremony. The instructions being given to us how to proceed, we commenced by asking several questions, but to these we received either no answers, or incorrect ones. The programme was this: We were to write down three names[4] of spirits, one of which was to be the name of the spirit we intended to invoke. We were then to put down the names of three diseases, one of which was to be the disease of which the person had died. We were then to put down three places, one of which was to be the place where the person died. We were then to point *seriatim* to the names of the persons, and that when we pointed to the name of the person intended, the spirit would signify his presence and approbation, by two raps, which mean YES. Names of others, or those not intended, would be answered by one rap, which meant NO. We made no progress, however, and, although there was an abundance of rapping, there was no communication, no intelligence, no

28

confirmation to us, of what we already knew (in the imperfection of human knowledge), and we appealed with an air and tone of assumed *naïveté* to the rappers to know if perhaps our failures were not owing to our great wickedness? "Oh, no!" said the Mother Fox, "it will happen so sometimes." Just then a gentleman entered who, it appears, was a devotee of Rappism, and a daily worshipper at the Fox shrine, for the purpose of holding communication with the spirit of a departed wife. As we had failed, entirely, to elicit even a respectable *guess* in answer to our inquiries of the spirits, and this gentleman had been more highly favored, his visit was rather fortunate at this juncture, for it gave us an opportunity to observe more closely than when our minds were occupied with the manipulation of the *spiritual telegraph.*

Mr. * * * commenced at once with an account of his previous interviews and then proceeded to inquire for his beloved spirit. Rap, rap, indicated her presence, and he asked some several questions which were answered to his satisfaction, the Fox mother repeating over and over the alphabet, so fast that we could not follow to get the answer for ourselves, but the rappers being in good *practice*, seemed to find no difficulty in keeping pace. We saw in this individual, a degree of infatuation rarely to be met with in intelligent *men of the world*, and unmistakable evidence of entire mental hebetude upon this particular subject. We,

29

however, turned his fascination to a very good account, as we shall presently show. We inquired if these rappings ever occurred any where except immediately about the persons of these girls. "Oh yes," was the mother's answer, "the sounds have been made in that wardrobe, and upon the door," etc. We pressed hard to have the raps from the wardrobe, but to our surprise and disappointment the girl got into the wardrobe, leaving the door open, and so snugly was she encased there in consequence of a partition in the wardrobe, that her dress was largely in contact with three sides or walls of the little apartment. Of course we did not expect any better or different performance from that with which we had been entertained outside the wardrobe. "Will the spirit rap here?" says the girl, and rap, rap, it came on the floor of the wardrobe. She was then requested to have the rappings made upon the sides and back of the wardrobe, which she did, taking a little extra time to arrange herself for these performances. She then requested us to put our ear to the top of the wardrobe and the rap would proceed from that quarter. We were not to be entrapped by this trick, for we knew full well the old and trite experiment of placing the ear upon one end of a long stick when a sound is made upon the other end. In this experiment the sound will always appear to be made near the ear. We therefore kept our attention fixed upon the bottom or lower part of the wardrobe, and while some present, misled by the artifice, supposed the sound came from the upper part of the wardrobe, we observed that the sound was produced where it was at first, down below, and that it was not modified in the least, which certainly ought to have been the case, if the sound had been made opposite to the person's ear. The girl then called attention to several points in the upper part of the wardrobe, and it appeared to the satisfaction of some present that the sounds came from those points, while to us it was perfectly evident that the sounds were not at all changed in direction or character, and in reality proceeded from the old quarter. Our knowledge of ventriloquism also fortified us against this trick. Ventriloquism is a deception, the success of which depends upon a certain power of modulating the voice, a correct ear for imitation of sounds, and skill and judgment in selection of time, place and circumstances for the performance. When persons present are not aware or apprised of the attempt to deceive them, the ventriloquist is not obliged to be very particular in his selection. But when his intention is announced or anticipated, his art is exercised to direct the attention of his auditors to the quarter from which he wishes the sound to appear to come. If our readers will turn to Brewster's Natural Magic on this subject, they will find many interesting tricks described on this principle. Nothing is more easy than to deceive completely, by calling the attention of persons present to sounds from a certain position or direction, while in reality the sounds are made elsewhere and in a remote quarter, provided the real origin of the sounds be concealed from the sight. So it was in the case of the raps, with those whose eyes and *expectations* were fixed upon the top of the wardrobe. The trick was poorly done however, for the sound did not undergo the proper modification, and in fact it was out of the girl's power to modify it to suit this case. For the origin of the raps, being concealed under her dress, she could not divest it of its muffled character without exposing her art. It is particularly worthy of note here, that for these experiments in the wardrobe no particular spirit was invoked, and the raps were continued as long as necessary for the gratification of the bystanders, and were several times commenced without any particular invocation on the part of the girl, she evidently forgetting the dignity of the spirit in the excitement of the moment. This over, it was desired to have the spirits knock at the door, but they could not manifest without the girl's immediate presence, and accordingly, she placed herself against the outside of the room door, which was about two thirds open, she taking hold of the latch. We were about to take position outside, in the passage, when she remarked that the spirits would rap much better if we took hold of the door. This was rather more necessary than cunning, and the rapper knew of course that unless she or some one held the door, the knock upon it would move the door on its hinges away from her. When she was fairly fixed with her dress in contact with the door, the raps commenced upon the door. After this she turned her head and asked if the spirit would please to rap in the passage, when she gave rather a feeble rap, which suited the trick tolerably well and here the rapping ended for this visit. The rap from the passage explained the purpose of keeping us in the room, for if we had gone into the passage the trick would have failed for us, as we should have been able from our position there, to refer the sound to the right quarter viz., about the girl's feet. On the second visit we were there with our former coadjutor and several other gentlemen of eminence, and a lady of the highest respectability, strong mind, and distinguished for her indomitable energy and perseverance. Our quondam enthusiast we found there at his matins, in company with several persons eminent in political life. One of them, a member of Congress, had been endeavoring to get some spiritual communications, but became so disgusted with the *bad guessing* of the Fox girls, that he left the room. The enthusiast, Mr. * * *, then invoked his favorite spirit and proposed a question, the answer to which was spelled out by the Fox mother as before, and he expressed himself perfectly satisfied with the answer. We then took our turn. We put down upon paper the names of three departed spirits, three diseases, and three places. In pointing to these names with the pencil, we took good care to conceal the pencil movement behind a book, and carefully

33

guarded against any emphatic movement which should betray our will to the practiced eyes of the girls. The raps came for the wrong spirit, and rapped the wrong disease, and place of death. We then made another effort. Three names were selected, as follows, Webster, Clay, and Calhoun; Webster's was the spirit we invoked, and they hit it right this time for the name, but mark the sequel. The answer was that Webster died of CROUP! and at Salem, Mass. Of course we did not indicate by any look or movement that our inquiries had been answered correctly or incorrectly until we had got through. Our scientific friend next made a trial, and his answers were more ludicrous if possible then those we had obtained. He attempted in several ways to get replies from the spirits, being always careful to give no clue to his thoughts by outward signs, but all to no purpose. The spirits, judging from the raps, were there in abundance, but no intelligence, or correct answers could be had from them. Next another friend of ours came to the trial. He had not been accustomed to investigate such tricks, and very imprudently suffered Mr. * * * to put the questions for him. The answers came in accordance with the facts, that is the right spirit was designated by the raps, and the manner of his death. Mr. * * * put the questions each in different tone and shape, and the girls undoubtedly read him as they had done before. Noticing this, we remarked to Mr. * * * that as he had been so successful we would like to have him inquire for us, to which he readily assented. We, however premised, that he must use the same *intonation* and *language* in asking each question, which he agreed to do, as far as he could. This we exacted, not because we had any suspicion of collusion in this case, but as we explained it at the time, because many persons would unwittingly by emphasis or some significance indicate to the rappers, or any shrewd person, the particular object he had in view. With these precautions, the question was put to the rappers. We were to fix our thoughts upon a particular spirit, the disease of which the person died, and the place where; the name with two others was put down upon paper, the disease with several others, and also the place of death with two others. Mr. * * * propounded as follows: Will the spirit inform us of the spirit the gentleman is thinking of? Rap, rap! Yes. Will it inform us correctly? Rap, rap! Yes. Pointing to a name with a pencil, he asked, Is it this? Rap! No. Is it this? Rap, rap! Yes. Pointing to the diseases and places, with the same question each time; when the whole was gone through with, Mr. * * * asked, Has the spirit informed us correctly? Rap, rap! Yes. We were thinking of Webster's spirit, and the result was this. The rappers hit it right as to the name, but they informed us this time that Mr. Webster died of FUNGUS HÆMATODES, in Newark, New Jersey.

This was too much for forbearance, but still we kept our purpose of investigation in view, and again pleaded our own wickedness as the probable cause of these failures. "Oh! no," said they, "it will happen so sometimes." What a deeply disgusting spectacle! These girls and their mother sitting there, with all gravity, and pretending to be the "*mediums*" of communication with disembodied spirits, and dealing out such nonsense as that just related.

The rappers were then sitting some distance from the table, and we asked if the "Spirits would rap upon the table?" Rap! No. "Will the spirit *please* to rap upon the table?" Rap, rap, rap. "Not now." It seems that three raps for the expression "Not now" was a part of the spiritual stenography, as they had occasion to use this evasion quite often to escape difficulties. "Will the spirit please to explain why it will not rap upon the table?" Rap, rap, rap! "Not now." "When will it?" "This evening, at such an hour," naming it. This last communication was spelled out by the Fox mother, and a time was named at which it would be impossible to get an opportunity to propound such a question, as they held their spiritual levee in the evening to crowds. Moreover, we had no desire to repeat the question to these tricksters, to be shuffled, as we most certainly should have been, with the same prevarication. On the occasion of our first visit, Mr. * * * said that the spirits had rapped upon his foot, while sitting at a table. The experiment was repeated by request, and very likely would have been successful, if we had not fixed our eyes very intently upon his and the rappers' feet. As it was, this feat was not performed. On the second visit, we implored the spirits to rap upon our feet. "Not now," was the answer. It was evident that we were not receiving our money's worth of spiritual manifestations according to the show-bill; but, as every failure was our gain, we were not disposed to quarrel with the rappers or the spirits. One of my scientific friends then asked if they would not rap if they were suspended in a swing, or stood upon a pillow? "Oh yes," was the reply, "we have done that; that has all been tried." One of the Fox girls proposed to send upstairs for a pillow, but it occurred to us that they *might* rap while standing upon any *common-sized pillow*, for the reason that their dresses would cover and extend beyond the pillow, and thus give them an opportunity to get their rapping instrument down upon the floor over the sides of the pillow. We therefore proceeded immediately, while they were engaged in some conversation, to make up a cushion upon the floor to suit our own views. We gathered a number of cloaks, and laid them folded upon the floor, so as to make a circular cushion of about three and a half feet diameter, and so thick that we were persuaded no ordinary raps with their instrument could be heard through the soft mass, or if any sound should be produced it would be so modified as to betray its origin. The Fox mother objected to this preparation; but the girls said, "We know we can rap; the spirits will rap there, for they have always done so." By way of an excuse for making this cushion, we remarked that one of the coats was silk, and that we would ascertain if electricity had any thing to do with it. The Fox mother said, "All that had been tried before; and that the girls[5]could rap standing upon glass tumblers, and that she knew it must be the spirits, for these manifestations had been with them now for six years." We replied (to keep up our argument), "You know that there are persons who think these sounds are all due to some modification of electricity, and others who think that electricity is the very essence of spirituality,[6] and we wish to see in this case how far it may be concerned in the phenomena." There was no resisting this, and we were allowed to proceed. The result was exactly as we anticipated. While standing upon the cushion *they could not rap at all.* The principal rapper saw her predicament, and took her stand upon the cushion so that her dress was partly over the edge of the cushion, but this we objected to, and requested her to stand upon the centre of the cushion, upon the plea that if her dress touched the floor, it would conduct away the electricity. A perfectly empirical reason, of course; but they were none the wiser for that, and as soon as every thing was arranged to our liking, she invoked the spirit to rap. No rap came. Again and again the spirit was besought, but no response was given. She then asked her sister to come and stand upon the cushion with her, thinking, in her subtlety, that two of them would occupy so much room as to give one, at least, a chance to have her dress over the edge of the cushion. But this we were prepared for; and gathered in the skirts of their dresses upon the cushion, upon the same plea as before. The result was the same as with one. No raps. The fact was, their arts were completely baffled, the spirits had fled, and the experiment not only proved the falsity of the assertion that they could rap standing on cushions, or when suspended in a swing, but afforded the most conclusive evidence of the immediate and wilful agency of these Fox girls in producing these sounds.

Thinking to redeem themselves from the inevitable verdict of this trial, the principal rapper proposed to stand upon glass tumblers, to see if the spirits would rap then, as they had done on former occasions. She took her stand upon the tumblers. This elevated the lower border of her dress above the floor, and it so happened that one of our number was sufficiently far from her that he could have seen her feet on the rapping instrument. She invoked the spirit. "Will the spirit please to rap?" No rap. She then stooped a little, as if addressing the spirit below. "Will the spirit please to rap now?" No rap. She then stooped a little more, and by this time her dress was fairly down upon the floor, so as to cover feet and tumblers. "Will the spirit please to rap now?" Rap, rap. This was very adroitly done, but the trick was clear to us. How strange it is, that she should have been obliged to stoop, and to have invoked the spirit three times before the answer came; and, moreover, that she should look down to the floor for the spirit; and how passing strange it is that these modern spirits should have such a fondness for *long dresses* and *girls' toes*. We then requested her to stand upon a chair, and rap. This she did promptly, and the rap came at a bidding. The sound was different from that produced upon the carpeted floor, and underwent just the proper modification of a blow struck upon a hard, uncovered, wooden seat. Here we stopped, having seen quite enough of this game of "*Fox* and *Geese.*" Before leaving the room, one of the rappers requested our scientific friend not to publish them, and another stepped up to the lady present, saying, "You do not think that I have any machinery about me to make these sounds, do you?" We have it on the authority of this lady, who seemed determined to leave nothing untried to lead to the detection of this imposture, that she asked these rappers if they would consent to a private examination of their persons, and that they refused it positively, adding that if she had any doubt as to the reality of these spiritual manifestations she would have satisfactory revelations made to her in her bed-chamber five weeks from that time. This prophetic intelligence they rapped out for the occasion according to their own fancy and usual evasive duplicity in such cases. The five weeks have passed, but the lady has, of course, received no spiritual visitations as predicted.

Our readers are now ready to ask if we have discovered the machinery or instrumentality by which these girls make the sounds. In answer, we say that our investigation is conclusive that these sounds are entirely at the control of these girls, and that we have placed them in situations where they could not rap at all. And if, after all this, we have invented several modes by which the rappings can be made as successfully as by them, we think we have discovered enough. During each of our two visits, we noticed, by very cautious and careful inspection, one interesting and significant fact—that each rap was attended with a slight movement of the person of the rapper, and that a very distinct motion of the dress was visible about the right hypogastric region. While watching this point the girl noticed us, and immediately rose, went to the window, and dropped the curtain to darken the room, which was on the north side of the building, and full dark enough before. When she sat down she drew her shawl over this part of her person. This was on the first visit. On the second visit, we were soon discovered watching this movement again, and she rose and procured a shawl with which she covered her person as before. We do not pretend to decide that this movement had any direct connection with the instrument by which she rapped upon the floor; if so, it was very clumsy and awkward, for we have devised a mode of rapping that involves no such motion, and which we will shortly explain. It may have been that this movement was connected with the device for rapping upon the table. We are of opinion that

41

when they rapped upon the table, it was upon the under side of the table-top and not about their feet. They did not, and evidently could not, rap upon the table without sitting closely up to the table. If this conjecture, as to the rap under the table-top, is right, the movement we saw is easily accounted for. Be it so, or be it not, we have invented a contrivance which raps upon the under side of the table-top, and which involves precisely the motion we discovered. It requires but little exercise of ingenuity to contrive means of producing these sounds. It has been stated that a relative of these girls has made a public statement under oath, that they produce the raps with their toes, in a peculiar manner acquired by long practice. The public papers tell us that electro-magnetism has been employed to carry out this fraud. The snapping of the joints has been resorted to by another; and indeed we can easily imagine a variety of ways in which these sounds are, or may be produced. The Fox girls rapped upon neither of these plans. The sound was machine-like, and too loud for a sound that could be made by striking the naked or unarmed toe upon the floor, and entirely too loud for, and differing in character from, the snapping of the joints, and as to electro-magnetism, it was entirely out of the question in this case. The Fox girls visit the houses of strangers and rap always with the same ease every where. The raps are never remote from their persons but always directly about their feet, unless it be when they are sitting at the table, as we have before said, when the rap appears to be on the under side of the table-top, although we would not undertake to decide fully upon this latter point, as they would not allow us to choose our position so as to judge of the true direction of the sound; for as soon as my coadjutor looked under the table, the spirits decamped and we had no rapping. There are certain circumstances, under which no ear, however skilful and practised, can judge correctly of the position or distance where certain sounds originate. Such a case is exemplified in the common speaking tubes used in public houses and elsewhere. When you place your ear near the tube, the voice appears to be uttered close to the ear, though the person speaking may be at a great distance. The Invisible Lady is another instance, for a full account of which, see Brewster's work on Natural Magic. But the most remarkable illustration of this case is exhibited in the following manner. If you take an iron rod ten, twenty, fifty, or one hundred feet in length and strike it at one end, the blow is heard by a person having his ear close at the other end precisely as if the blow was struck near his ear. This illusion is more remarkable if the listener cannot hear the original blow through the medium of the air. To make the whole experiment very imposing, suppose an iron rod, three-fourths of an inch in diameter, projecting three or four feet through the floor of a large hall, and that this projecting part is a continuation of a rod passing beneath the floor of the room, and concealed entirely from observation and terminating out of doors, or in a distant apartment. Whenever a blow is struck upon the remote and concealed end, the sound not being heard except through the medium of the rod, appears to every person present, precisely as if it issued from the projecting end within the hall. With proper pre-concertion and ceremonial preparation, such a contrivance as this would far exceed, in mysterious character, the shallow trickery of these *feet-rappers*. From this experiment, which we have tried with entire success with a rod only twenty feet in length, we see how closely we must look to all the attendant circumstances and possibilities of the case, before we can conclude strictly upon the position of the origin of sounds, where their origin is out of sight. We know that the rapping was always about their *heels* when these girls sat in chairs, stood upon the floor, or in chairs, or stood in the wardrobe, or rapped upon the door. For this part of the performance we had abundant opportunities for examination, and if these girls will stand upon the floor and allow us to examine their feet, at the time of the rapping, we defy them and their spirits to produce the rappings without a full exposure. It is worthy of note that witches have always been far more numerous than wizards. There are reasons for such disparity in numbers, but this rapping business is particularly the province of females. There are no male rappers unless it be of late, since they have resorted to confederacy, or electrical or mechanical tricks. There are no men-rappers who rap upon such an extensive scale as the Fox girls. The latter are not confined to a certain table, a certain room, or certain spots in a room, or a certain house. They carry their "*Rattle-traps*" about with them, and go from house to house, and their "*familiar spirits*" are very sociable, unceremonious, and accommodating. If they will but adopt the Bloomer costume, our word for it, the spirits would signify their disapprobation by departing at once. Relying upon their sex they trust the courtesy of their visitors as sufficient protection against the examination of even their feet, and therefore they make bold to wear unusually long dresses the better to conceal their movements and rapping apparatus. When the girl stood upon tumblers, she did not venture to rap till, by gradual stooping, she brought her dress down so as to cover her feet and touch the floor. There are then special reasons why this kind of witchery should be played off by females. *The Fox style of rapping* CANNOT *be performed by men, or in the male attire.* We do not attribute to woman more or greater proneness, or power to deceive than to man; but when woman undertakes to deceive, she is generally more successful. She is less suspected, has fewer motives, runs greater risk, and incurs greater loss in the event of disclosures, and with the blandishments of person and sex, she silences opposition, smothers inquiry, defies and escapes

45

inspection, and lastly takes captive the head with the heart. Possessed of greater susceptibilities and easily impressed; she is more readily carried away by new and strange fascinations, and in times of certain remarkable developements of sympathetic witchcrafts, she is the first to be imposed upon and most apt to impose upon herself. This characteristic is well illustrated in the case of the *jerks*, a species of *witch mania* which prevailed in this country so extensively many years ago, in which women figured so largely. Sympathetic action is potential with both sexes, but especially with women does it overpower sense, reason and volition, giving rise to temporary insanity. We are however uncharitable enough to believe that, in many cases, upon these occasions the surrendry of the judgment and bewilderment of the imagination is not altogether involuntary, and that the whole operation of *being bewitched* might be arrested at a certain stage of its progress by an effort to resist, except perhaps in conditions of extreme hysteria and nervous prostration, or irritability. We have seen a young lady of the very highest respectability at a *table-tipping*, tugging away at the table to make it move, and all the while endeavoring to conceal her exertions, and declaring, when interrogated, that she did "not make the slightest effort." Can it be that she had become so infatuated as to forget that she was, or to persuade herself that she was not, deceiving, and yet all the while to be so assiduous and adroit in accomplishing her object? Charity says yes. Well! after all, there is something in the feat of deceiving and blinding reverend and grave Senators, Judges and Priests, well calculated to whet the pride, stimulate the cunning, and foster the love of power in a young Miss, especially when her arts are practised upon some doings not embraced in the criminal code nor amenable to law. There are probably— paradoxical as it may seem—cases of honest deception. The desire to accomplish something great, something exceeding the common course of familiar phenomena, may be so strong as to beget an entire perversion of all truthfulness, a self sanctioning of error, artfulness, and imposture, oblivion of conscience, an enthusiastic profession of faith and spirited advocacy of the new developments, a bending of every thing to conceal the fraud, and withal a remarkable preservation of the appearance of sincerity, and an air of ingenuousness so well put on as to appear natural, which go very far to inveigle those who may witness the performances.

Of the modes we have devised of producing rappings we will not explain more than one, that being sufficient to effect rapping sounds without disturbance of the person. We have contrived a great many, and although we have not seen the particular mode employed by the Fox girls, yet we can rap just as well. A piece of soft metal such as lead, shaped like a *chain shot* or *dumb-bell*, tied to the great toe may be made to pound upon the floor, the door, the bottom of a wardrobe, or any surface or thing which may be under or about the feet, with forcible demonstrations. If any person will make the effort to move the toe up and down while the sole of the foot rests firmly upon the floor, it will be found that a considerable motion may be effected, and of course a *rapping*, without a disturbance of the person. A little practice will make perfect. In order to walk about without the rattling of the rapping piece, it is necessary to tie to one end of it an elastic cord, a piece of vulcanized rubber answering very well, and fasten this around the waist. A slight stooping or sitting down will leave the instrument free to work. If you have thin shoes or slippers on, it may be affixed outside of the slippers, or you can have it attached to the toe, and make the slipper large enough to slip over the whole and slip it off, when rappings are called for. One other element and we are all equipped for spiritual rappings; petticoats or long dresses are indispensable to complete the invention. Whatever be the contrivance adopted to rap upon the floor, the whole must be concealed within the sanctuary of *skirts* beyond the invasion of the curious or rude. We have other more perfect, better concealed rapping instruments than the one just described,[7] but not quite so simple or easy of application. Moreover the one described gives the double rap, (a peculiarity of the Fox contrivance.) These girls managed their instrument adroitly, and deserve some little credit for their ingenuity in contriving and operating an instrument so successfully as to baffle the scrutiny of thousands of their visitors. They walk freely about with their instruments, though a lady remarked to us that they both walked very awkwardly. With local preparations "*mysterious*" rappings may be produced in a variety of ways, but these girls, the *prototypes* of all rappers, neither employed or needed any aid from electro-magnetic motions, acoustic science, or confederacy to practise their arts, they used more ingenious and simple means. It is possible to make a rapping electro-magnetic movement, battery and all, small enough to be carried under the dress, but like the telegraph, it must be controlled by volition and muscular action of the operator, and where is the advantage of this over a mechanical instrument that raps directly? There is no necessity for wonderment or the taxation of ingenuity on account of these rapping sounds so long as you are excluded from a personal examination of the rappers. We wish very much that the civil authorities would pounce upon these rappers in the "*very act*" (*for obtaining money upon false pretences*)—(or some other plea) and make a forcible disclosure of their trappings. We believe that this can and should be done, and that such a proceeding would meet the full sanction of law and justice; that universal public opinion would sustain it, and we have no doubt of the nature and effect of the *denouement*. If it had already been done, we should have been spared the labor of this treatise at least, and we need not advert to the vast amount of suffering and vice that would have been forestalled.

Seeing then, that we can *rap*, yes, and give the double rap, how shall we account for the extraordinary prophecies, messages, coincidences and communications in accordance with facts? We wish this had been the only difficulty to surmount, for it perplexes much less than the *feminine security* of these rappers against the inspection of their actual *quomodò*. We can most safely presume that if by search warrant, stratagem, or *vi et armis*, the rapping instrument of these Fox girls had been exposed to the public, there would not have been one doubt about the nature and origin of the *spiritual communications*, nor the question ever asked, how it happened that these communications were so wonderfully true to fact. Brains, books, good and bad spirits, devils and all would not have been needed for this discussion. Indeed where is the necessity at all, of dragging out human weakness, credulity, and duplicity to solve the psychological part of this fraud and forgery, if we can rap as well as the Fox girls (the great guns of rappism), and on the strength of our rappings tell *more truth* and *fewer lies* than their spirits, what need have we of metaphysical disquisitions on the handwriting found in a drawer or any where else, resembling Mr. Calhoun's, John Smith's, or any other of the great departed?[8] So far as our experience went, the Fox girls made few, very few good hits, and perpetrated a vast amount of most intolerable nonsense and contradiction; enough of itself, even if the rappings had been made outside the pale of their *queenly robes* one inch, two feet, above their heads, in the aerial centre of the room, disconnected with every tangible and visible thing, to have turned any sensible man on his heel instanter, with contempt and disgust. But for the sake of those who are duped or perplexed by these communications, we must spend a little breath to enlighten them. When a man *suspects* supernatural agency or interference in physical, really visible, sensible, or tangible demonstrations, he is ready to believe any thing communicated at the time, and when he comes to the full belief in divine interposition, his faith is perfected. Where, by long practice, preparation and skill, tricks are performed with a view to imposition, it requires the highest degree of coolness, calmness, and self-possession, to resist the impression of the superhuman, and however well fortified we may be in these respects, it is hardly to be expected that we should be able to discover the real nature of the performance without some experience and practice on our side. The instant the idea of the superhuman gets possession of the mind all fitness for investigation and power of analysis begins to vanish, and credulity swells to its utmost capacity. The most glaring inconsistencies and absurdities are not discerned and are swallowed whole, and so deep is the blindness and so extraordinary in its

51

character, that we have seen a convert made to *spiritual rappism* upon the strength of one single coincidence selected from among a great mass of disgusting mummery and perversion of truth. Not one of the discrepancies, were of any importance with him; one lucky hit of the rappers and the whole performance, errors, raps and all were invested with supernatural power. Now, how does it happen, that the believer in such cases does not notice the incongruities and failures, or does not appear to notice them. This is somewhat of a psychological phenomenon, but might as well be explained on the ground of unfairness, as any other; unfairness is as often the beginning and accompaniment of *infatuation*, as a mental incapacity for more than one idea. A shrewd person can, at any time, take a promiscuous company, and with the imposture of rapping, or any other trick, calculated to divert the attention, and a mode of spelling out communications similar to that adopted by the Fox girls, make out as many or more wonderful and seemingly supernatural communications as they, certainly not more of error and absurdity. We were once riding in a stage-coach, with a gentleman, who, after a long journey, laid a wager with another that he would tell the occupation of every person in the coach. To the surprise of all he won the wager. A lady present, apparently much hurt, asked how he knew she was a "housekeeper." The reply was, Because I saw you frequently putting your hands to your belt—for the keys. Many of our shrewd itinerant phrenologists, after the parade of measuring and fumbling one's head, and a few master-key questions, will portray the life and character with a wonderful degree of accuracy. Our stage-coach pythonist had, during the journey, watched the motions, complexion, conversation, expression of countenance, appearance of the hands, the dress,—in fine, ever little circumstance of habit or person, and it so happened judged rightly in each case. It is so with the phrenologist, who draws his information mostly from similar sources.[9] It is so with the rappers; they observe carefully, have experience with persons of all classes, and generally, unless molested by some skeptic, have every thing in their own way. Their visitors, especially the dupes, betray more to these rappers than their own skill can eliminate, and it is surely to be expected that they should hit right sometimes. Upon mere hap-hazard conjecture, this might happen occasionally, but with all the arts and aids of preparation, credulity, and fanaticism, they become as successful as the oracles of Delos and Lesbos.

Before concluding the subject of rappings we remark briefly that a SPIRIT that cannot or will not tell the truth on all occasions, is wholly unworthy our credence or respect; and believing, as we do, that miracles are God's prerogative and all miraculous power is withheld from evil spirits as militating with the plan of Revelation, we needed no further investigation for our own satisfaction, than to know that a very large part of their pretended communications were grossly erroneous; but we have held it to be important for the sake of others that the whole subject should be examined. The fever has somewhat abated of late, but unless boldly and vigorously assailed it will reappear under some new pretension with exacerbations more virulent than ever.

FOOTNOTES:

[1] This witch of Endor it seems was the only woman with a *familiar spirit* that had escaped death under the royal edict of Saul, and how successfully she bewitched or juggled Saul our readers all know. We refer them one and all to the 19th Chap. Leviticus, 31st verse—ED.

[2] In Washington.

[3] The Bible teaches of witches and wizards with familiar spirits, and that they were to be put to death; of magicians, astrologers, sorcerers, soothsayers, and false prophets; but the only account of a miraculous performance by the devil, is that of his first great and momentous fraud upon our race in the garden of Eden, and this is by some considered as allegorical. Through that act he got possession of the human heart, and he needs now no external manifestations to further his intrigues.

Pharaoh's magicians were able, by their arts, to imitate to a certain extent only, the miracles of Moses and Aaron. They turned their rods into serpents, the river into blood, and caused frogs to come out of their hiding-places, but when it came to the conversion of the small dust into lice, their magic was baffled, and "then the magicians said unto Pharaoh *This is the finger of God.*"

The raising of Samuel's spirit, and his prophecy of the result of the battle, was a professional trick of the witch of Endor, and no more remarkable than many of the doings related of the rappers and tippers, and of mesmerizers who send clairvoyants to explore the UNKNOWN WORLD. Considering all the circumstances, we think that many hits, or conjectures of false prophets, or fortune-tellers of the present day, have been quite as successful, and even more wonderful, than this feat of the witch of Endor. We know that some Commentators regard the raising of Samuel's ghost, and the prophecy of the result of the battle, as the work of God, and not of the witch herself, or her master; and to such a conclusion they seem to be forced, if they admit any thing superhuman about it, for it would not answer to accord so much power to a witch, accursed of the law. How such an explanation can be reconciled with Divine attributes and teachings, we are at loss to conceive. The account tells us that Saul had sought the Lord in vain. The Lord had refused to communicate with him. Shall it be said then that the Almighty is capable of trifling? (for this seems to be the alternative.) That he made known his will through a witch; and that, in Saul's (the Lord's anointed) last extremity, the Lord forced him to believe a lie or an accursed witch? Is not this the inference, the inevitable conclusion? How readily all difficulty vanishes by expounding this transaction upon the very same principles that we apply to spirit-rapping, viz.: that it was a juggle, and like all witchcraft of whatsoever kind, was of human immediate instrumentality. To affirm of such performances that they are inexplicable, and amazing, is no argument in favor of their superhuman character. They are not more wonderful or difficult of explanation, than hundreds of tricks which we see, and of which we read every day, as performed by jugglers. To the great mass of mankind these latter are equally puzzling, and would undoubtedly pass for miracles, were it not for the fact that they are *professedly* tricks. We believe in the all-pervading, all-controlling, all-sustaining power of God, in Divine interposition, special Providences, and the efficacy of prayer, as taught in the Scriptures, after our own interpretation. *We believe that miracles are God's prerogative, and believing thus, we conclude that the working of miracles by the devil, or evil spirits, would furnish an excuse for man's unbelief or infidelity.* Most earnestly, therefore, do we deprecate the advancement of any theory (for it can be but *theory* at the best), which attributes these and kindred delusions, to the direct agency of the devil, or evil spirits. Such teachings are mischievous in their tendency, and militate with the true interests of Christianity, just as far and as long as they have no better foundation than theory, speculation, or conjecture, and are wanting in proof positive, invincible and overwhelming, of their correctness.— C.G.P., Ed.

[4] We were thus given to understand that spirits retain their earthly names, and answer to them. It occurred to us, therefore, that if we put down the name of John Smith we should be sure of a response.—C. G. P., Ed.

[5] The expression was very common with them that *"they could rap*, or *had rapped."* Rather careless, certainly!

[6] We, of course, had no more thought of electrical agency here than in the rap of an auctioneer's hammer.—C.G.P., Ed.

[7] We have made excellent rappings with this instrument, and accompanied them with very wonderful communications.—Ed.

[8] Whatever respect we may have for the memory of the great, we feel at liberty to banter their spirits if we catch them in bad company, and at base tricks.—Ed.

[9] We believe in the fundamental doctrines of phrenology, but have no faith whatever in this common empirical trade of delineating character promiscuously by the contour of the head alone.—Ed.

TABLE-TIPPINGS.

This fallacy demands our most rigid scrutiny, and none the less of severe reprobation, from the fact that it is engaged in, to a great extent, by respectable and intelligent persons. The business of Spiritual Rappings is a sheer and miserable imposture, and as the performers are obliged to invent and manage the machinery, or whatever instrumentality produces the sounds, there is no possibility of their deceiving themselves. The table-tipping is rather a case of delusion, or self-imposition, though there are occasionally actors in this performance who betray insincerity, and some whose actions give the *lie direct* to their professions. How it happened that TABLES were selected for the demonstrations of departed spirits, or the operations of the "*new fluid,*" is beyond our wisdom to explain. Why should not the pump-handle work *sua sponte*, the cradle rock itself, or the coach start off without horses, as well as tables jump about the room at the mere imposition of hands, or the behest of those wonderful personages entitled *mediums*? Is there any thing in the shape, material, purpose, or history of a table that it should become, *par excellence*, the connecting link between the natural and the spiritual world? or that it should be the great reservoir of electricity, magnetism, "*new fluid,*" "*od,*" or what not? Perhaps *legs* are indispensable to this new species of dancing and jumping. But, as in many of the best *authenticated* cases, the table moves along the floor with a gradual, slow, and dignified motion, without jumping, and more especially as many of the tables are upon castors, we see no reason why wheels should not be better than legs, and why coaches will not do as well, or better, than tables— for the rolling friction is much less than the sliding friction, and carriages could be made very light for this particular purpose. These tipping magicians are not very fruitful in expedients or they would have attempted long ago the speculation of a *new line of spiritual coaches on common roads, propelled by mediums.*

But to the point. One of the first table-tippings that came under our notice was one which had become quite celebrated, and of which we had heard a great deal before we came to witness it. We were informed, by persons of high intelligence, who had been eye-witnesses, and participated in the experiments, that when several persons joined hands around this table, in connection with the medium, the table began to move about the room with force, celerity, and apparent life. That forcible resistance could not stop it, and that the performers were hardly able to keep up with its motion. That, on the same occasion, heavy bodies were lifted from the floor by the mere superposition of hands, without grasping; in other words, that by laying the hand upon a heavy article, and raising the hand, the dead weight *lifted itself* from the floor, and followed the motion of the hand.

Our informants were men of high standing, of high endowments and general intelligence, men of veracity, and men whose opinions were worth much in legal questions and matters of state. Oh! what a discovery and development was here. ADIEU YE LEVERS, SCREWS, WEDGES; PULLEYS, SCREW AND LEVER-JACKS, CRANES AND BOOM-DERRICKS, STEAM, GAS, AND EVERY KIND OF ENGINE, HORSE AND ALL OTHER POWERS, FIRE, AIR, AND WATER, ELECTRICITY AND MAGNETISM, CHEMICAL, MECHANICAL, AND ALL SUBSERVIENT AGENCIES, ONE AND ALL, ADIEU! Mind has subverted the laws of matter; all philosophy is merged in spirituality, and volition has become the all-potent, all-sufficient, all-pervading power; the crazy and pitiable seekers after perpetual motion are become the master spirits of the age, and gravity and friction have given way to two new controlling principles, levity and non-resistance. Suffice it to say, we laughed at our informants, and gave them a flat contradiction, "that they had not seen what they related." It is well worthy of remark here, that we have never yet known any one of our acquaintance to take serious offence at the most positive contradictions upon this subject,—a proof, to our mind, that there is a secret, deep-seated, smothered conviction against the reality and genuineness of these manifestations. A curious element of our composition it is, that honest men find no little difficulty in deceiving themselves, and take so little or no umbrage at being charged with this kind of deception.

60

Imbued deeply ourselves with an ardent *penchant* for novelties upon every subject, and a determination to *ferret out* the extraordinary pretensions of this new wonder, we have taken occasion to inquire of persons, from all parts of the country, where these exhibitions have been made, and we assure our readers that although the time may thus have been profitably spent, the inquiry became tedious even to disgust. We heard substantially the same story from all; viz., that the tables tipped and moved about "without visible agency," and yet, in almost every case, upon close sifting and careful cross-examination, we found that somebody had hands upon the table during the whole of its gambols. Surely the *devil has to do with table-tippings*, for we have never seen honest-minded persons so unfair and oblique on any other subject before. Not that the fiend tips, kicks, or propels in any way the tables, but that he tips either the conscience or the judgment to a deplorable extent to sustain the cheat. In every inquiry and investigation we have found gross and weak exaggeration, and have fully resolved that we will maintain, to the last extremity, the position of unqualified, uncompromising denial and opposition, to the *highest testimony of earth*, as to the verity of *table-tippings, spirit-rappings, or any kindred chicanery of miraculous or spiritual purport*. We were much gratified recently at the remark of an experienced friend, that "he would not believe these things, even if he saw them with his own eyes." There was meaning

61

in the remark. He would not admit the testimony of others to such an anomaly, and he would not trust or believe *himself* if he should give way to the conviction that all of mathematical and mechanical science, all of religion and bible teaching, and all of common sense, was to be contravened and exploded by these new manifestations, promising endless perplexity, confusion, crime, and insanity, and no good to any body. Our friends repeatedly say to us, "we don't see how these things can be, but we cannot discredit the opinion and testimony of Mr. A., Dr. B., Prof. C., Rev. Mr. D., Judge E., Hon. Mr. F., &c." "We think it hard to impugn such testimony, and why should not their word in this matter go as far as yours?" Our plain answer is this: if we tell you that black is white, and white is black, we do not expect our testimony to be regarded; and we take the same privilege in repudiating all testimony, from whatever source, of a similar character. It was a strong, though reverential, position of St. Paul, that "even an angel from heaven would be accursed if he preached any other doctrine than that which he, Paul, had preached," for he well knew that an angel from heaven could not preach any other.

With all reverence we say it, we feel a sort of inspiration upon the laws of reaction, gravity, and friction, based upon the experience of every moment of remembered life, that compels us to reject peremptorily the testimony of our best friends, of the most distinguished and credible persons, or of the most exalted intellects, when they tell us that by the mere superposition of hands, or by the effort of the will, a table moves off by itself, or lifts itself from the floor without visible agency. There are several individuals in this place, ourselves among the number, who have agreed to give two thousand dollars to any person who will show to us such a feat performed by a table. We feel entirely safe in the offer, and moreover think it prudent, in case we should deposit the money, to deposit it in a Savings Bank paying interest, for otherwise the money might be lying idle for a whole lifetime. We might hesitate, if there were the remotest chance of explaining such extraordinary appearances upon any principle of science; but the fact is, these assertions contravene all science, and bear absurdity on their very front. We hear some say, gravity, electricity, and magnetism cause bodies to move without visible agencies or connection. Yes! they *do*; they always *have*, and always *will*. But here, in the year of our Lord one thousand eight hundred and fifty-three, we must be told, for the first time, that the human body has analogous powers to magnets and thunder-clouds; and, more than this, that no regular law of traction or attraction, propulsion or repulsion, governs this marvellous, new, nervous, corporeal, carneous power, *odylic* force, or what not, but that it is subject to all the anomalous, capricious and vicious directions and governance of *human* volition.

We have too much contempt for *odylic* philosophy, or any such chimera or vagary, to stop and discuss it here. We have for twenty years, ever since the revival of Slumbering Mesmerism, by Dr. Poyen, of Lowell, Mass., made diligent inquiry and patient, persevering effort to obtain from among the great mass of mesmeric performances some evidence of a new principle, new force, or any resolution of nervous or sensorial agency into physical power other than that of a mind upon its own body, and have never yet seen the most faint indications of any such nervous power as these modern psychologists pretend to unfold to us. What! a nervous force that acts exterior to, and independent of, its own tenement and rightful fulcrum? that propels masses heavier than the *body corporate*, without rending the latter in twain? Of one thing we feel assured, that this new-fangled philosophy is a poisonous, though covert fang, secretly gnawing at the very root of Christian faith. It made a bold sally in that coarse proposition of Miss Martineau respecting our Saviour's miracles—too coarse indeed to meet with favor—and now assails, under a less offensive and more sophistical garb, of "*odylic force*;" seeking to explain a mystery of the Bible (always an *infidel effort*), and to bring miracles and God's prerogatives within the scope and control of human reason and action. We ask any theologian who may incline to apply such tests to the solution of miraculous performance, if he supposes that if the mountain had removed, and been cast into the sea, at the bidding of the disciple (with faith as a grain of mustard-seed), that disciple would have been the source of the propelling power, and felt fatigue, depression, or reaction in proportion to the mass to be removed? If, when at the call of Joshua, the huge orb of earth stood still upon its axis, the vast momentum recoiled, through *odylic ether*, upon poor Joshua's brain? We can all accept the proposition of Archimedes *"Give me a place whereon to stand, and I will move the world;"* but who upon the largest latitude of plastic, ductile OD, or any other principle or pretext of mesmeric sophistry, would venture to arrest and propel the earth by the odylic, nervous, sensorial agency of one of its little creatures, held to its centre by indomitable gravity. Perchance it may be reasoned that from Joshua's cerebral fountain there issued a vast stream of odylic essence, or psychological fluid, whose mighty gushing into space was equal to the momentum of huge earth, and reacting, like water in the mill-wheel, caused the great sphere to stop. Oh! how hazardous, yea impious, is the attempt to *explain* a miracle—God's prerogative, God's interposition in former times, though not above human *command* upon the touchstones of prayer and faith, yet always and *forever* above human *ken*. Our Saviour himself said, "Of myself I can do nothing," and his miracles were prefaced with prayer. GOD of the Bible! while thy word stands, the wisdom of the wise and prudent shall not prevail over the faith, simplicity and common-sense philosophy of thy "Babes."

It is painful and humiliating to see the efforts of certain prominent men publicly advocating the genuineness of these manifestations, and especially so when we consider the character of the assertions and arguments brought forward in support of their doctrines. One of the most recent and striking is this. Mr. Calhoun's spirit on being consulted through the Fox mediums as to the object of these spiritual manifestations, replies, that they are "instituted to prove to the unbelieving the IMMORTALITY OF THE SOUL, and to propagate peace and harmony among men."[10] Hear it, all Christendom, believers, readers and hearers of the WORD! The great conflict and triumph of the Gospel is to be crowned by the deductions of these new FOX THEOLOGISTS, or, rather, as a more legitimate inference, the Word of God is to be superseded and must now give place to the higher manifestations of Rochester spirit-rappings and table-tippings. It is no less than a denial of the sufficiency of revelation for the very purpose for which it was intended, and denying this it denies the whole. All other reasons, arguments, developments, experiments, doubts, suspicions and manifestations aside, this rapping and tipping theology has now taken a decided and hostile stand against the BIBLE, and as such it must be treated. Hear it, and mark it well! The Bible is discarded as plainly and fully as if it had been uttered in so many words. In vain does Holy Writ every where teach of the immortality of the soul, in vain are its maledictions against sorcery and witchcraft, in vain does it pronounce "Anathema Maranatha" against additions to its divine pretensions, in vain its precept "that no prophecy of Scripture is of private interpretation," in vain does it declare that an unbeliever "would not believe though one rose from the dead,"[11] in vain have been the Bible societies, missionary and all the mighty efforts to spread Christianity, ALL is to be blotted out before the new light of "*Rochester knockings*" and Fox legerdemain. But why should we indulge in appeals, tirades, irony, or satire, knowing all the while that we have positive demonstrations yet to present of the utter fallacy of table-tippings; proofs irrefragable of the mundane, mortal, corporeal, physical, muscular character of table-tippings? We have our reasons. If we are to encounter fools and fanatics, witches and wizards, devils and dupes, we must assail in every vulnerable quarter, for even demonstrations of fact are sure to be denied upon some impudent pretext, and in such cases facts are not all-puissant weapons, and require an auxiliary guard. With the candid and the wavering, however, our demonstrations will be appreciated, and we trust conclusive. Reverting to the first case of table-tipping that came under our notice, having heard much of the extraordinary performances we went in company with a scientific friend to see for ourselves. The medium was a sprightly young girl, whose reputation for sincerity might have been her dearest treasure. The wonderful feats of this medium were recounted to us, and we longed for the verification. After a brief conversation, she with another young lady, (about half medium) placed hands upon a small table, our friend joining the circle. Their hands were so placed, that the right hand of one concealed the left hand of the other. After a while, the table began to move. This was natural, certainly, for we noticed that this medium was working very hard with her concealed hand to move it. Perhaps her mother saw this, for she rose from her seat and said, "You are not tricking, now?" "No, indeed, mother, I'm not tricking; see how lightly I *press*!" What a comment was all this upon the recital just made by her mother to us of the astonishing feats of moving heavy dining-tables, tearing up the carpets, moving pianofortes, &c.! Our friend beginning to suspect the voluntary character of this motion of the table, made a counter effort with his fingers (better concealed than that of the medium for the reason that he was possessed of far greater strength), and the table stopped moving. But this was not all. We detected upon the countenance of the medium an expression of disappointment, and further, a more palpable striving to move the table, in consequence of this resistance, which she seemed not to suspect. All this seems too farcical to relate, and yet the *superhuman* performances of this very medium had been described to us by eye-witnesses of the highest respectability as marvellous, and astounding in the extreme, and our principal informant was a gentleman well known for his astuteness, had some years back published an excellent work upon mathematics, and was as well qualified as the average of learned men to observe and decide upon such matters. His testimony was confirmed by several others, all witnesses of the highest respectability, and what was it all worth? and what is all other testimony worth upon this *aerial vaulting* of tables? Perhaps we are mistaken as to the effort made by this medium to move the table. Let us see! We placed a sheet of paper on the table under her hand, and as soon as the table was desired to move, behold the sheet of paper moved over the table-top, while the table stood still. Here is the demonstration of this fallacy, and although in such a shape that it may be cavilled at, yet it is, however, the elementary key, and to us all-sufficient in itself. We will, however, develope it in such form as to be beyond all cavil. We witnessed, after this, many abortive attempts by mediums and others to move tables, and some other attempts that began to succeed, till we applied our mechanical tests, when the new fluid, electricity, magnetism, nervous power, odylic force, all resolved themselves into muscular action, and the tables never moved unless clearly pushed. As to tables moving in *any way* without being touched, we repeat that it has never been done, and challenge proof to the contrary.

69

Fig. 1.

We have traced up many such exaggerations, and invariably found the story to be that the mediums were not moving it, but *merely* had their hands "*lightly*" upon it. After we had baffled the tippings by the sheet of paper, we were on another occasion told, that paper was a non-conductor of electricity, and that if this agent had any thing to do with it, the paper might intercept the action. Willing to indulge the whim we substituted for the paper the instrument represented in Fig. 1, well known as the parallel ruler. It is simply a flat ruler (*a*), furnished with four rollers (*b*) (*b*), upon which it rests. The slightest pressing forward of the fingers upon the ruler (*a*) causes it to glide easily forward upon the table. Of course the result was the same as with the paper. Upon invoking the spirits, or exerting the will, the ruler moved upon the table, while the table stood fast. If, then, the *paper* moved, and the *ruler* moved, ought we not to infer that the friction between the fingers and the paper or the fingers and the ruler was greater than the friction between the paper and the table or the ruler and the table? Certainly. It must be remembered here that the rule of tipping is, to press or touch *very lightly* with the fingers. Ought we not to infer that the paper and the ruler were pushed by the hand, since the hands followed them in their motion? Certainly, upon the common doctrine of touch and go; but these new philosophers will not allow us even this inference, and maintain that the odylic power moves both hand and paper. A most versatile, vicarious agent or power is this OD. Well, odd as it is odd, we have given the tippers full swing, and we now administer their *quietus*. Fig. 2 is an illustration of our mode of annihilating odylic power and a positive cure for the *malady of spiritual medium*. Let the bodies of the tippers or mediums be fastened or restrained from motion in any way back or forth, and then let their arms be stretched straight out, as shown in the figure, and their hands locked, superposed, or placed in any way they please upon the table. Sitting with the breast closely against the back of the chair is a convenient way of restraining the forward motion. Now let them invoke the spirits, exert the will, let them cry out and howl, Belial won't come, the table won't move, for all the mediums of earth, and passive matter holds true to her law of inertia. If the table should be moved towards them, it will be seen that if the arms be kept straight, the hands keeping their position, will appear to move over the table. We take some credit to ourselves for this discovery, and we have been much surprised that men of science, men of mechanical minds who have witnessed table-tippings have never thought to apply some rule or test of mechanics to solve this mystery.[12]

Fig. 2.

The very first thing to arrest our attention in table-tipping was the fact that the hands (no matter how lightly they pressed) moved always with the table back and forth; and this suggested at once our mechanical tests. How strange it is that any mortal in possession of his senses, should move a table, and not know it! And yet it is so, it has been so, but, we trust, it will be so no more. If any medium or tipper can gainsay this demonstration, we should be glad to hear from him, and would like to employ him, at a high salary, as a mechanical agent, to overcome for us, in a multitude of ways, the operations of gravity and friction. The traders and merchants generally must have a care of these tippers; for, in buying and selling, they can tip the scales with more ease than tables. We have, however, no doubts as to the results, if any one will try these experiments fairly. It will be a cause of chagrin to some of those honest-minded tippers, who have all along been believing that the spirits tipped the table, and that they were in reality holding communion with their departed friends. If we prove the table-tipping to be the result of a muscular movement, we need not dwell upon the psychological phenomena of the extraordinary coincidences, messages, &c. They are all referable to that peculiar condition of mind, INFATUATION, under which judgment is suspended, memory quickened, sensitiveness exalted, imagination predominant, and involuntary actions induced.

In concluding this work, we remark that our investigations have fastened error, mercenary motives, imposture, and illusion upon those doings, so far as they have come under our observation. Our opportunities have been of the best kind as respects the rappings, for they were with the Fox girls, who were the leaders in this whole business of rappings and tippings; and, suffice it to say, we effectually prevented their rapping.

When error and falsehood are driven from one subterfuge they soon find another; and as the *surveillance* of truth and science approaches their hiding places, they resort to more covert retreats; and these girls may hereafter contrive some new mode of rapping not explicable upon our theory, but it is enough for us to know that it will be still a trick. We have had as wonderful performances related to us as have ever been heard of elsewhere; but, upon close sifting; they have all proved to be within the pale of human conception. Doubtless all these tricks will assume different shapes from day to day and place to place, and the performances in England, France, and Germany, may all differ from ours and from each other. The tricks *must improve*, in order to sustain their pecuniary value, or bolster reputation; and however successful and impenetrable they may become, they are none the less tricks, and have one common origin.

If any one deems that he hath a spirit, or any new power beyond jugglery, let him come, and we will welcome him with a close examination; and if we are baffled, and cannot make our position good, he shall have the reward we have specified in a previous part of this work. Those who make these tricks their profession have the advantage of long practice, preparation, and confederacy; but let them come and claim the prize, if they will and can.

We have recently heard of some refined tricks at table-tipping, in which other preparations were made than the mere superposition of hands. Although we had rather see them than hear of them, we have only to say to those who may see them (or think they see them), Divest yourselves of all idea of the supernatural, or any new fluid, or new law, or property whatever, and, regarding the performance either as a trick or case of illusion, scrutinize sharply every movement and circumstance in connection, and you will find that either the table does not move, or, if it does move, you will see what actuates it. Remember! there are controlling and controllable agents that *can* raise a table from the floor; but the action of the will, or the mere superposition of hands, NEVER!

THE END.

FOOTNOTES:

[10] A recent conspicuous writer, in giving an account of this great communication from the great spirit of Mr. Calhoun, says, its spiritual character was confirmed by the rising of the table from the floor, and other wonderful signs.—C. G. P., ED.

[11] The actual reappearance of dead Dives, *in propria persona*, was declared by the Almighty as inadequate to convince unbelieving Jews; but it seems that for Gentiles the presence of the spirit without the body is all-sufficient.—ED.

[12] These experiments were made in February and March, 1853, and, since the above was written, we are pleased to find that Faraday has taken the matter in hand, and pursued a course of investigation similar to our own.

CONTENTS

SPIRIT-RAPPINGS... 3

   FOOTNOTES: 54

TABLE-TIPPINGS. 58

   FOOTNOTES: 75